Magi—magic.
What comes to mind?
Riches?
Mountains of glittering gold, silver,
or precious jewels?
Spells and potions, enchantments,
castles, or curses?

Or maybe, you think of Love—of
Wisdom.
Here is a story, of little matter perhaps,
but one I wish to relate.
Of two children.
Of Christmas.
And of the meaning of Magi—magic.

THE GIFT OF
THE MAGI

Illustrated by
Robert Sauber

Adapted from the story by
O. Henry

The Unicorn Publishing House, Inc.
Morris Plains, New Jersey

What could possibly be done? One dollar and eighty-seven cents. That was all. And sixty cents of it was in pennies. Poor Della had scrimped and saved for an entire year with this result. Three times Della counted it. One dollar and eighty-seven cents. And the next day would be Christmas.

There was clearly nothing to do but flop down on the shabby little couch and howl. So Della did it. All her hard work. For nothing. All her pretty plans. Ruined. A present for Jim, her brother, the most important person in her life—that's all she asked. A present for Jim.

Della finished her cry and went to the dresser to powder her face. She gave a little sigh and turned to look out the back window. She stared blankly out the window at a gray cat walking a gray fence in a gray backyard. Tomorrow would be Christmas Day, and she had only one dollar and eighty-seven cents with which to buy Jim a present. Many a happy hour she had spent planning something nice for him. Something fine and rare and sterling—something just a little bit near to being worthy of being owned by Jim.

How everything had changed! And it always seemed for the worst. There had been happier days. They felt so very far away now. She could just barely remember Christmas Eve two years past. Papa had to work late. Papa always had to work late. Mama had been in the kitchen since early morning, cooking and preparing the Christmas dinner. Jim had found what most certainly was the best tree in all the city, and he had struck a good bargain besides. They spent the entire afternoon decorating the tree, Jim and she.

When Papa finally arrived—all was ready. What a wonderful Christmas! The food. The songs. The presents. The family. But that was all gone now. Papa was gone. Mama was gone. A lot of people died that winter. That horrible, cold winter. Jim and she had been on their own ever since. They had made out all right, despite the hardship. Jim had been good to her. They had been good to each other.

And now another Christmas was here. Della had worked all year out of the little four-room apartment, when there was work, as a seamstress. She would sew garments long into the night, usually by candlelight, as she counted on the savings in gas fuel towards Jim's present. Jim worked as a clerk in a bank, where he made twenty dollars a week. They made a living. Yes. But that was about it. Expenses always seemed greater than their hard won efforts. Life had asked a lot from the fifteen-year-old girl and her sixteen-year-old brother. But Della would not be denied. There must be something that could be done. Something that she could do. She was determined to make Jim's Christmas the best it could possibly ever be.

Della went back to the dresser and sat—deep in thought. She gently pulled her hair down to its full length and stroked the soft strands with a brush. As she ran the brush through the long, smooth locks, a smile (just a tiny wisp of a smile, at first) came to her lips. It grew. It became a full-blown grin. Ear to ear. Della knew in a moment just exactly what to do.

Della jumped up from the chair and ran to the mirror. There she stood, turning slightly from side to side. Pulling her hair back from her shoulders, she let the long strands fall rippling and shining towards the floor. It reached below her knee and made itself almost a garment for her. She stood still for a moment, admiring its luxury.

Now, there were two possessions of Della and Jim's in which they both took a mighty pride. One was Jim's gold watch that had been their father's and their grandfather's before. The other was Della's hair. To both, it would take more than any king's ransom to wrestle from them such beloved treasures as these. But as Della stood before the mirror, her eyes shone with such a brilliance that no amount of gold or silver could ever compare.

Della did her hair up again nervously and quickly. Once she faltered for a minute and stood still while a tear or two splashed on the worn red carpet. But just for a minute.

On went her brown jacket; on went her old brown hat. With a whirl of skirts and with the brilliant sparkle still in her eyes, she fluttered out the door and down the stairs to the street.

When she finally came to a stop the sign read: "Mme. Sofronie's Hair Salon. Hair Goods of All Kinds." Della hesitated, then entered. There before her stood Madame Sofronie, quite large, very pale, and with a chilly expression that hardly looked "Sofronie."

"Will you buy my hair?" asked Della.

"I buy hair," Madame said simply. "Take yer hat off and let's have a look at it."

Della removed her hat and down fell her beautiful hair. All the ladies in the salon eyed her with envy.

"Twenty dollars," said Madame, as she lifted the mass of hair and carefully eyed the soft locks.

"Give it to me quick," said Della. Madame took up her favorite pair of scissors and it was over. The women in the salon never spoke a word. A hush fell over the place. Everyone in the salon clearly mourned the young girl's loss. Everyone, that is, except Madame.

For the next two hours the shopkeepers in town held their breaths as a frenzied whirlwind passed in and out of their shops. Della was ransacking the stores for Jim's present.

She found it at last. It surely had been made for Jim and no one else. There was no other like it in any of the stores, and she had turned all of them inside out. It was a platinum chain. Handsome and simple in design, displaying its value by substance alone—as all good things should do. It was even worthy of The Watch. As soon as she saw it she knew it must be Jim's. It was possessed of only the purest qualities. Quietness and value—like Jim. Twenty-one dollars they took from her for it, and she hurried home with the eighty-seven cents. With that chain on Jim's watch instead of the worn leathern strap that now held it, Jim would be properly anxious to give the time in any company.

Along the way, Della stopped. Snow had begun to fall. Big fat flakes. Big fat lazy flakes—that took their own good time as they floated about here and floated about there, before finally settling to the earth. She was standing outside a toy shop, looking in. Della was becoming a young woman now, most certainly, but she had not all together forgotten the joys of childhood. Not yet.

Within the frosty windows could be found all the dreams of youth. A fat teddy bear. A laughing clown. A china doll. And best of all, a merry-go-round. A mechanical merry-go-round. Della watched as the tiny horses went up and down, and round and round, to carnival music. She could just barely hear the tune the little toy piped so gayly. She pressed nearer the glass. She was very close now. But the music seemed so very far away. So distant. Almost as if . . . Della quietly turned away and walked down the white streets for home.

When Della reached home her joy over Jim's present was tempered a bit by common sense. She lit the gas and took out a curling iron. Setting herself to work, she began to repair the damage made by her generosity and her love. Within forty minutes her head was covered with tiny, close-lying curls. She looked at her reflection in the mirror long, carefully, and with a touch of sadness.

"If Jim doesn't kill me . . . " Della said to herself, "or worse, he might laugh me to tears. Oh, but what could I do—what could I do with a dollar and eighty-seven cents!" Della drew a deep breath and let out a deeper sigh. Then she lit the stove and made some tea. Jim would be home soon.

Jim was never late. She heard his step on the stair of the first flight, and she turned white for just a moment. Della had the habit of saying little silent prayers about the simplest everyday things, and now she whispered: "Please God, let him not be unhappy when he sees me."

The door opened and Jim stepped in and closed it. He looked thin and serious. Poor fellow, he was only sixteen—and to be burdened with so much! He was in great need of a new overcoat and a pair of warm gloves.

Jim stopped inside the door. He didn't move an inch. His eyes fixed upon his sister, with a look that held neither anger or surprise, or even disappointment. Just a blank, far-off kind of a look. The kind of look a person has when they think they have forgotten or lost something of importance.

"Jim, please," Della cried, "don't look at me that way. I had my hair cut off and sold it because I couldn't have lived through Christmas without giving you a present. It'll grow out again—you really don't mind, do you? My hair grows awfully fast. Say 'Merry Christmas!' Jim, and let's be happy."

"You've cut off your hair?" Jim said dully, half to himself, as if the fact was unable to enter fully into his mind. Then he stared about the room as if Della's hair might magically appear at any moment.

"You needn't look for it," Della said. "It's sold, I tell you—sold and gone. It's Christmas Eve, Jim. Be good to me, for it went for you."

Jim woke from his trance, and drew a package from his overcoat and threw on the table.

"Don't make any mistake, Dell," he said, "about me. There's nothing in the world that would make me think any less of my sister. But if you'll unwrap that package you may see why you had me going a while at first."

Della was so excited. Her nimble fingers tore at the string and paper. And then screams of delight and joy. And then, sorrow! A flood of tears and wails flowed from poor Dell, that it was some time before Jim could calm and soothe his sister.

For there lay The Combs—the set of combs, side and back, that Della had worshipped for so long in the store window. Beautiful combs, with jewelled rims— just the color to wear in her long, beautiful hair. The hair that was gone. They were expensive combs; of that she knew. Oh, how her heart had yearned over them without the least hope of ever having them for her own. And now, they were hers, but the hair they would have adorned was not.

But she hugged them close to her, and at length she was able to look up with dim eyes and a smile and say: "My hair grows so fast, Jim!" Then she jumped and let out a little cry. With all the fuss she had almost forgotten. Jim's present. She hadn't given Jim his present.

Della eagerly held out the beautiful chain in her open palm. The dull precious metal seemed to flash with a spirit almost as bright as the joy in Della's loving eyes.

"Isn't it a dandy, Jim? I hunted all over town to find it. You'll have to look at the time a hundred times a day now. Give me your watch. I want to see how it looks on it."

Instead of obeying, Jim tumbled down on the couch and put his hands under the back of his head and smiled.

"Dell," he said, "let's put our Christmas presents away and keep'em a while. They're too nice to use just at present. You see, I sold the watch to get the money to buy your combs. And now suppose I give you a hand at making Christmas dinner. I'm starved!"

The magi, as you know, were wise men—wonderfully wise men—who brought gifts to the Babe in the manger. They invented the art of giving Christmas presents. Being wise, their gifts were no doubt wise ones. And here I have lamely related to you the uneventful tale of two foolish children who most unwisely sacrificed for each other the greatest treasures of their house. But in a last word to the wise of these days let it be said that of all who give gifts these two children were the wisest. Of all who give and receive gifts, such as they are wisest. Everywhere they are wisest. They are the magi.

For over a decade, Unicorn has been publishing
richly illustrated editions of classic and contemporary
works for children and adults. To continue this tradition,
WE WOULD LIKE TO KNOW WHAT YOU THINK.

If you would like to send us your suggestions or obtain
a list of our current titles, please write to:
THE UNICORN PUBLISHING HOUSE, INC.
P.O. Box 377
Morris Plains, NJ   07950
ATT: Dept CLP

❖❖❖❖

Printing History 15 14 13 12 11 10 9 8 7 6 5 4 3 2 1

Library of Congress Cataloging-in-Publication Data

    The Gift of the Magi / illustrated by Robert Sauber ; adapted from a story
the story by O. Henry.
    p. cm.
    Summary: A brother and sister sell their greatest possessions to buy
Christmas gifts for each other.
    [1. Christmas—Fiction. 2. Gifts—Fiction. 3. Brothers and sisters—
Fiction.] I. Sauber, Rob, ill. II. Henry, O., 1862-1910. Gift of the Magi.
    PZ7.G3636 1991
    [E]—dc20   91-7313
                                                                CIP
                                                                AC